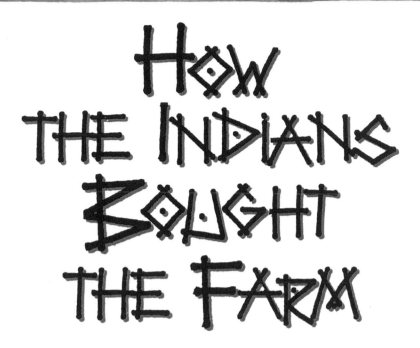

How the Indians Bought the Farm

By Craig Kee Strete and
Michelle Netten Chacon

Pictures by Francisco X. Mora

Greenwillow Books, New York

Watercolor paints were used for the full-color art. The text type is Della Robia.
Text copyright © 1996 by Craig Kee Strete and Michelle Netten Chacon
Illustrations copyright © 1996 by Francisco X. Mora
Printed in Hong Kong by South China Printing Company (1988) Ltd.
First Edition 10 9 8 7 6 5 4 3 2 1

Library of Congress Cataloging-in-Publication Data

Strete, Craig.
How the Indians bought the farm / by Craig Kee Strete and
Michelle Netten Chacon ; pictures by Francisco X. Mora.
p.   cm.
Summary: A great Indian chief fools a government man into believing
that a wooly bear is a sheep, a beaver's wet nose belongs to a pig,
and the rumble of running moose is that of cows.
ISBN 0-688-14130-7
[1. Domestic animals—Fiction.   2. Animals—Fiction.
3. Farm life—Fiction.   4. Indians of North America—Fiction.]
I. Chacon, Michelle Netten.   II. Mora, Francisco X., ill.   III. Title.
PZ7.S9164Ho   1996   [E]—dc20
95-5464   CIP   AC

For Gil, with my love and respect always, and
for my brother Derek, a most extra-special person—
I think of you every day
—M. N. C.

To my nieces, Yoya and Diana
—F. M.

In days not so long ago, a great Indian chief and his great Indian wife lived on the homeland of their people. A government man came and told them to move.

"You must live here and farm, and then everybody will be happy," said the government man.

At the new place, there was a wooden house and wooden barn. "If you are to keep this farm we gave you, you must raise sheep and pigs and cows," said the government man. "Lots of them."

"We don't have any sheep or pigs or cows," said the great Indian chief.

"We don't have any money to buy sheep, pigs, or cows," said the great Indian wife.

"That's not my problem," said the man. "But you will be in big trouble if you don't get some."

"We must find some animals to live on this farm," said the great Indian chief to his wife. "Or we will be in big trouble."

"If you ask me, we already *are* in big trouble!" answered the great Indian wife.

And she was right.

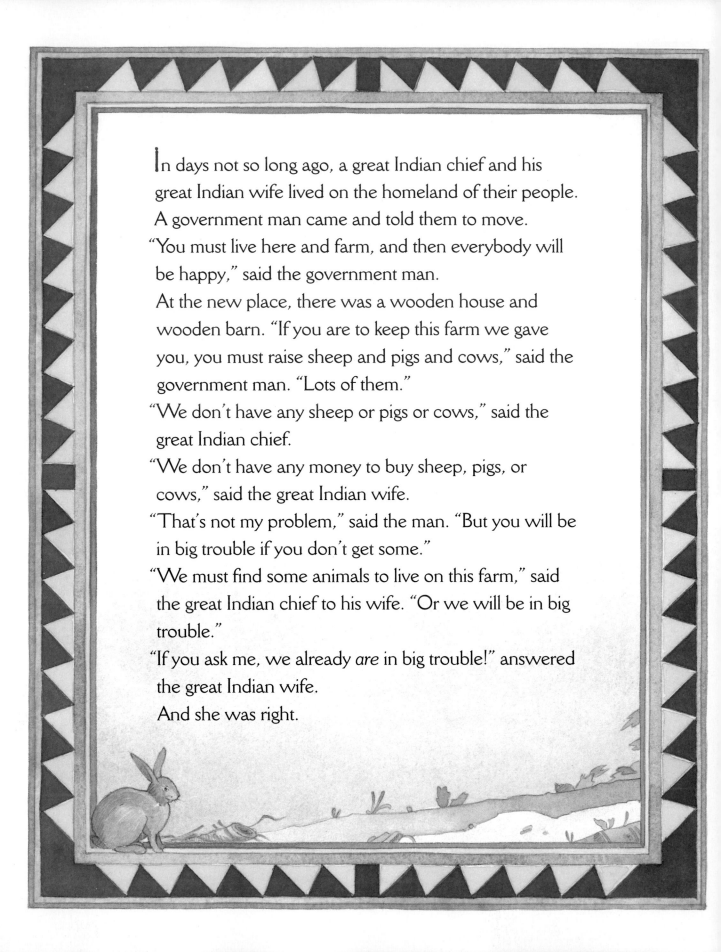

Near the house, behind the barn, flowed the great river. The great Indian wife said, "If you take your canoe down the great river, perhaps you will see cows and pigs and sheep that are wild and do not belong to anyone. Perhaps you will see them living along the great river."

The great Indian chief knew his wife was very clever,
so he got into his canoe early one morning and went
paddling down the river.

He paddled a very long way and saw lots of cows
and lots of pigs and more sheep than he could
possibly count.

But they all belonged to somebody.

He paddled around a big bend in the river. He saw a brown moose eating twigs on the river bank.

"Hello, brown moose. You are a wild animal and no one owns you," said the great Indian chief. "How would you like to come home with me and eat things better than twigs? I will feed you the finest grass."

"That sounds good," said the brown moose, and he got into the canoe.

It was a very big moose and a very small canoe.

The great Indian chief paddled on down the river. On a spot along the river bank where a great oak tree grew, he saw a brown beaver eating bark.

"Hello, brown beaver. You are a wild animal and no one owns you," said the great Indian chief. "How would you like to come home with me and eat things better than bark? I will feed you the sweetest-tasting wood I can find."

"That sounds good," said the brown beaver, and he got into the canoe.

It was a medium-sized beaver, but the canoe seemed even smaller now.

They paddled on. At a place along the river where the water runs very deep and small fish are always jumping, the great Indian chief saw a brown bear catching one of the fish.

"Hello, brown bear. You are a wild animal and no one owns you," said the great Indian chief. "How would you like to come home with me and eat things better than tiny fish? I will feed you the biggest, juiciest fish I can find."

"That sounds good," said the brown bear, and he got into the canoe.

It was a very large brown bear.
The canoe sank like a stone.

So brown moose, brown beaver, and brown bear walked
all the way back to the great Indian chief's farm. They even
had to carry the great Indian chief part of the way because
he got tired.

He put the animals in the barn. His great Indian wife came out to see them. The great Indian chief gave an armload of grass to the brown moose and said, "This is our cow. See how he eats grass."

The great Indian chief gave a bucket of wood chips to the brown beaver and said, "This is our pig. See how he eats wood chips."

The great Indian chief gave a big fish to the brown bear, but his wife spoke before he could say anything. "And this, I suppose, is our sheep!" She shook her head sadly. "Well, I guess that's the best we can do. But nobody ever had a sheep that ate fish."

"This is very good grass," said the moose. "The best I've
ever had."
"And these wood chips are like no others," said the beaver.
The great Indian chief looked at the brown bear.
"More fish, please," said the bear.

"Listen," the great Indian chief said to the animals. "The Great White Father has told me I must have many animals for my farm or I will lose it. And I do not have them. But I can grow the best grass, chop the best wood chips, and catch the juiciest fish."

"We have friends," said the moose. "Lots of them. We will go and bring them here."

The great Indian chief went into his house and
told his great Indian wife, "Soon we will have many
animals on our farm."
"Cows and pigs and sheep?"
"Not exactly," said the great Indian chief.
The great Indian wife looked worried.

One night a week later, there was a knock on the door. It was the government man again with a thick stack of paper in his hands. He had several other men with him, all dressed in green uniforms. Nobody smiled.

"It says on these official papers that you will have to move again," said the man. "You promised to raise sheep and pigs and cows, but you don't have any!"

"Not in the house," said the great Indian wife. "We keep them in the barn."

"Are you saying that you have sheep and pigs and cows?" asked the man, looking very surprised.

"In the barn," said the great Indian chief. "But I wouldn't go out and look at them now if I were you. I just fed them, and they don't like to be disturbed when they are eating."

"I don't believe you have pigs and cows and sheep!" said the man unpleasantly, and he waved the official papers at them. "We'll just go and see for ourselves!"

The government man and the men in green
uniforms rushed outside. The man with the
papers and the great Indian chief went into the
barn. "We will wait out here," the men in green
uniforms said.

Loud noises and chewing sounds came from all
around, but it was dark.
"See?" said the great Indian chief. "They are eating."
"Turn on the light," said the man.
"I don't have one," said the great Indian chief. "But
the sheep are over here. Feel their woolly coats."

The great Indian chief led the way. He knew
where to go even in the dark.

The man stuck his hand out and felt thick, soft,
woolly hair. Lots of it.

"Your sheep are very woolly," he admitted. Then
he heard many big growls. The man snatched
his hand back. "I never heard of sheep that
growl."

"I told you they don't like to be bothered when
they are eating," the great Indian chief explained.

He led the man to the next stall. There was a great sound
of wood crunching. "Here are my pigs," he said.
The government man did not want to, but he put his hand
out and felt a wet nose. Then he felt sharp teeth.
"Ouch!" he cried. "Your pig bit me."
"I keep telling you they want to eat in peace. Leave them
alone, and they will not growl or bite," the great Indian
chief said patiently.
"I'm getting out of this dark barn," the government man said.

"Where are your cows?" he demanded.
"Where are your men in green uniforms?" asked
the great Indian chief.
"They are hiding under the wagon," said the great
Indian wife, pointing. "I think they are afraid of our
sheep and pigs."

"We are not afraid!" shouted the man, very
angry now. "And I asked you before, *where
are your cows?*"

"In the pasture, of course. They are eating.
Do you want me to call them?"

"Yes!" said the government man.

"Very well," said the great Indian chief. "But they will not be happy about it."

The great Indian chief stamped on the ground and then waited. "They are coming," he said. "And they are not happy." In the distance, a rumble was heard. And it grew louder and louder.

The men in green uniforms were not under the wagon anymore. They were running away as fast as they could go.

The government man's face was whiter than his white papers.
"Here they come," said the great Indian wife. Suddenly, big
brown shapes came running out of the forest.
"They are really mad," said the great Indian chief.
"As mad as can be," agreed his wife. "They might trample our
barn down. Or worse."

"Do you believe us now?" asked the great Indian chief.

But the government man was gone, leaving only his tracks behind.

The great Indian chief and his great Indian wife never saw the
government man again. But that was fine with them. They were
busy enough just taking care of all the animals on their farm.